MYSTERIES IN HISTORY

What Were the Pyramids?

Solving the Mysteries of the Past

Charlie Samuels

Cavendish
Square
New York

Published in 2018 by Cavendish Square Publishing, LLC
243 5th Avenue, Suite 136 New York, NY 10016

Website: cavendishsq.com

© 2018 Brown Bear Books Ltd

Cataloging-in-Publication Data

Names: Samuels, Charlie.
Title: What were the pyramids? / Charlie Samuels.
Description: New York : Cavendish Square Publishing, 2018. | Series: Mysteries in history: solving the mysteries of the past
| Includes index.
Identifiers: ISBN 9781502627988 (library bound) | ISBN 9781502627995 (ebook)
Subjects: LCSH: Pyramids--Egypt--Juvenile literature. | Egypt--Antiquities--Juvenile literature. | Egypt--Civilization--To 332
B.C.--Juvenile literature.
Classification: LCC DT63.S265 2018 | DDC 932--dc23

For Brown Bear Books Ltd:
Editorial Director: Lindsey Lowe
Managing Editor: Tim Cooke
Children's Publisher: Anne O'Daly
Design Manager: Keith Davis
Designer: Lynne Lennon
Picture Manager: Sophie Mortimer

Picture Credits:
Front Cover: Ricardo Liberato (http://liberato.org)/Wikimedia Commons
Interior: Ancientart: 18; **Dreamstime:** icon72 33, Janino 47; **Public Domain:** 4, Marco Almbauer 27, Art Renewal
Center/Hearst Castle 39, Supreme Council of Antiquities 44l, Ronald Unger 25, Waters Art Museum 23, Yorck Project 8;
Robert Hunt Library: 21, 35, 38; **Shutterstock:** Leonid Andronov 1, 5, BasPhoto 19, Dan Breckwoldt 10, Francisco Bucchi
42, bunhills 43, Francisco Caravana 12, Everett Historical 36, FineShine 28, Jaroslav Moravicick 22, Morphart Creation 11,
Eugeny Sayfutdinov 9, Fedor Selivanov 13, Cory Sober ifc, 7, Maxar Tamal 40, Sphinx Wang 44-45, Vladimir Wrangel 41,
Mikhail Zahranichny 20; **Thinkstock:** Hemera 24, istockphoto 16, 17, 29, 30, 31, 32, 34, Photos.com 14, 15, Plus99 6;
U.S. Navy: 26; **Waters Art Museum:** 23.

Brown Bear Books has made every attempt to contact the copyright holder.
If you have any information please contact licensing@brownbearbooks.co.uk

All websites were available and accurate when this book went to press.

Manufactured in the United States of America

CPSIA compliance information: Batch #CS17CSQ.

Contents

What's the Secret of the Pyramids?... 4

Who Built the Pyramids?.................... 12

What Did the Egyptians
        Believe About Death?.................. 20

Who Was Buried Inside the Pyramids?...28

What's Left to Discover?.................. 38

Glossary... 46

Further Resources 47

Index 48

What's the Secret of the Pyramids?

Thousands of years ago, ancient Egyptian workers constructed the pyramids, some of the largest structures ever built. But how and why did they build them?

There are about 100 pyramids in Egypt. They all stand on the west bank of the Nile River. The oldest are over 4,000 years old. Some are little more than piles of rubble. At Giza, however, three huge pyramids still rise above Cairo.

The pyramids at Giza stand outside Egypt's modern capital city of Cairo.

The Great Pyramid at Giza was the tallest human-made structure in the world until the 1300s. All the Egyptian pyramids had a square base. Four triangular sides sloped up from the base to meet in a point. Each pyramid was topped with a **capstone** that pointed directly up to the sky.

Pyramid Building

The pyramids stand along the Nile River in Egypt. Some are grouped closely together. They were built near the capitals of Egypt. The capital city moved as different families took control of ancient Egypt. The pyramids all stand on the west bank of the Nile, because people were thought to travel to the west after they had died.

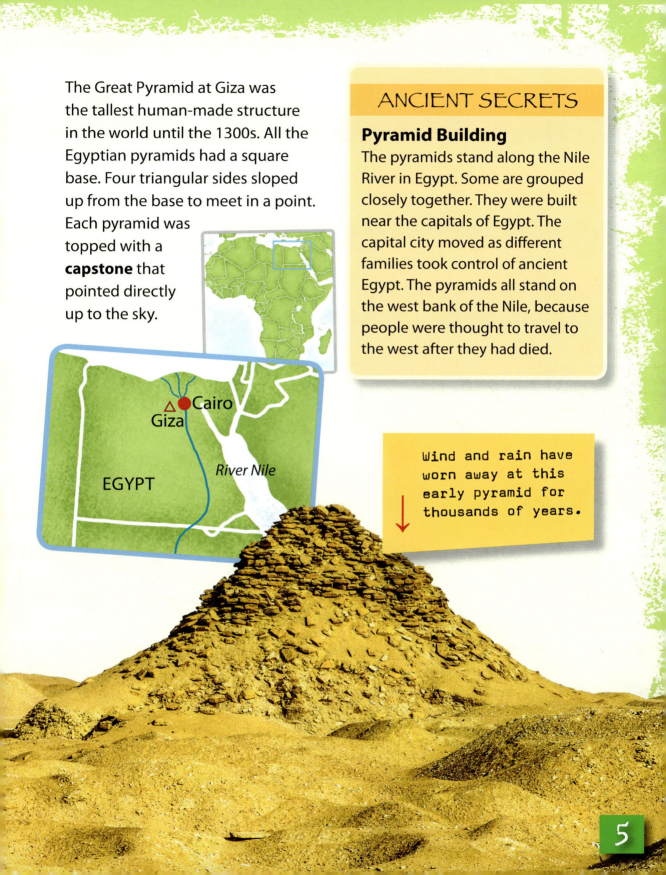

Cairo
Giza

River Nile

EGYPT

Wind and rain have worn away at this early pyramid for thousands of years.

Kings and Gods

What was the purpose of these huge structures? Other cultures also built pyramids. Some were used as temples. Others were used as points that helped to track the movement of objects in the night sky. In Egypt, however, experts have discovered that the pyramids were built as tombs for kings.

The ancient Egyptians believed that their pharaohs, or kings, represented the gods on earth. The Egyptians thought the gods lived in the sky. The pyramids needed to be tall enough to help dead kings return to the sky. With the technology the ancient Egyptians had, the tallest structure they could build was a pyramid. The pyramid shape also represented the sun's slanting rays. Ra, the sun god, was the most important god in ancient Egypt.

The Great Sphinx of Giza has a man's head on a lion's body. It guards the pyramid of Khafre.

ANCIENT SECRETS

Djoser's Step Pyramid

The first pyramid was built at Saqqara for a pharaoh named Djoser (reigned ca. 2630–2611 BCE). It was built in a series of steps. Each level was smaller than the one below. At the top was a rounded peak. The pyramid was built by an architect named Imhotep. It was around 200 feet (60 m) high. The step pyramid still stands today, although some of its bricks are crumbling.

Djoser's pyramid has six levels and is made from stone and mud bricks.

What's Inside?

For centuries, people wondered what the pyramids might hold. Most pyramids were built between 2600 and 1800 BCE. After that, the pharaohs were buried in the Valley of the Kings in Luxor. By around 1400 BCE, even Egyptians had forgotten why the pyramids were built.

Around that time, Pharaoh Thutmose IV ordered workers to clear the site of the Great Pyramid of Giza. They dug into the sand and revealed what is now called the Great **Sphinx**. It is a massive statue of a lion's body and a human head. The statue is probably meant to be the pharaoh Khafre. It guards his tomb.

The Arabs Arrive

Thutmose's workers did not go inside the pyramids. It was centuries later before anyone explored the interior of a pyramid. In 642 CE, the Arabs conquered Egypt, which became an Islamic country. Muslims from Asia and Africa began to visit the pyramids. They wondered what might be inside. Were the pyramids full of treasure?

In ancient paintings, the god Ra was shown as having a bird's head with the disk of the sun above it.

↑ Ruins of ancient temples stand along the Nile River throughout Egypt.

Into the Pyramid

There was only one way to find out. Around 820 CE, the Islamic ruler of Egypt, Caliph al-Mamun, decided to break into the Great Pyramid. He ordered his workers to light fires to heat the stones of the pyramid. Then, they poured cold vinegar on the stones. He hoped this would crack the stones open.

The stones did not crack, so the caliph's workers dug into the side of the pyramid. They tunneled about 100 feet (30 meters) inside, but found nothing and were about to quit. Then, they heard movement, as if something was dropping. That meant there must be a space inside the pyramid. They dug toward where the sound was coming from. Suddenly they broke into a passageway!

Two Chambers

The Arabs named the tunnel they found the "Descending Passageway," because it led downward. They found another, known as the "Ascending Passageway." The diggers also found two chambers. The first held a large granite **sarcophagus**. This chamber is known as the King's Chamber. The second, smaller chamber is called the Queen's Chamber.

Three smaller pyramids stand next to the huge pyramids at Giza.

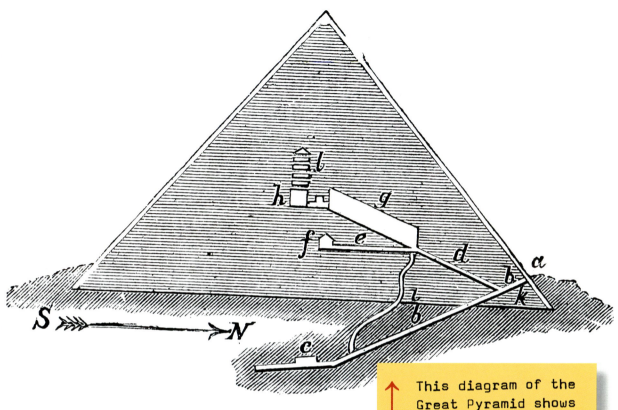

This diagram of the Great Pyramid shows the King's Chamber (h) and the Queen's Chamber (f).

The **vaulted** ceiling of the second chamber reminded the workers of the chambers where Muslim women were buried. Although the diggers assumed it belonged to a queen, no sign of a queen has been found there.

The One and Only

Today we know that the Great Pyramid was built for Pharaoh Khufu. The pyramid is unique. It is the only Egyptian pyramid to have an internal structure of passageways and rooms. Before the Great Pyramid was built around 4,500 years ago, no pyramid had any corridors or rooms. After Khufu's pyramid was completed, no other pyramids were built this way. No one knows why.

Who Built the Pyramids?

The Egyptian civilization in the Nile Valley lasted for over 3,000 years. What do the mysteries of the pyramids tell us about the people who built them?

Ruins of ancient temples and palaces still stand along the Nile River. Over the centuries, experts have found many objects that help explain how the Egyptian people lived. Society was divided into nobles, workers, farmers, and slaves. Clues about how they lived come from pottery, jewelry, clothes, paintings, weapons, toys, and musical instruments.

The Nile River was the major highway in ancient Egypt.
↓

Egyptian Writing

One of the best sources of information is Egyptian writing. The Egyptians used picture writing called hieroglyphics. Each symbol could stand for the thing it depicted or for a sound. Hieroglyphs were carved or painted on the walls of pyramids and temples.

For centuries, nobody knew what the hieroglyphs meant. The first clues to understanding them came from another kind of Egyptian writing. This was called Demotic. It was quicker to write and easier to read than hieroglyphics because each character stood for a single sound, like letters in a regular alphabet. The Egyptians wrote in the Demotic script on scrolls of papyrus. Papyrus was a form of paper made from the fibers of reeds.

A Powerful State

Egypt's rise to power in the ancient world began centuries before the first pyramids were built. In around 3100 BCE a pharaoh named Narmer united two kingdoms. They were Upper Egypt in the south and Lower Egypt in the north.

The new state of Egypt began to conquer its neighbors. It became a powerful trading nation. Its ships sailed as far as the east coast of Africa. Egypt's power started to fade after 1000 BCE as its neighbors grew stronger. It was still rich, however. It continued to trade with Asia and Africa. Egyptian farmers in the Nile Valley grew so much grain there was enough to trade with Egypt's neighbors.

Foreign Enemies

Egypt's wealth attracted enemies. Many different tribes tried to take control of the kingdom. Around the 1400s BCE, a group known as the Sea Peoples invaded Egypt. They may have come from the eastern Mediterranean. The Libyans and Nubians also took power in parts of Egypt at different times. In 30 CE the future Roman emperor Augustus defeated his rival, Mark Antony, and Antony's partner, the Egyptian queen Cleopatra VII. Augustus took control of Egypt for the Roman Empire.

ANCIENT SECRETS

The Rosetta Stone

The Rosetta Stone was found by French soldiers in Egypt in 1799. It declares a new law of Egypt's King Ptolemy V in three languages. At the bottom is ancient Greek. In the middle is Egyptian Demotic. At the top, the message appears in hieroglyphs. Scholars hoped the stone would help them understand hieroglyphs for the first time. It did, but the code still took over two decades to crack.

↑ The Rosetta Stone is on display in the British Museum in London, England.

More than 90 percent of Egypt was desert, but its farmland was very **fertile**. Every year, the Nile River floods over the fields along its banks. The floodwaters leave behind nutrient-rich black **silt**. As early as 5500 BCE, the Egyptians began growing wheat and barley. They used water from the river to **irrigate** the fields. They saw the annual flood as a symbol of magical rebirth and the generosity of the gods.

SCIENCE SOLVES IT

Reading the Hieroglyphs

Experts studying the Rosetta Stone used the Greek text to figure out the other languages. In 1802, they found five place names in the Demotic text. That was the first step in learning to read the script. The hieroglyphs were more difficult to understand. They mixed up pictures that stood for things and pictures that stood for sounds. A French scholar named Jean-François Champollion finally cracked the code in 1822.

Farming People

Agriculture was at the heart of life. Every farmer had to give some of his crops to the pharaoh. If there was a **drought**, the pharaoh gave out this grain to make sure everyone had food. Farmers sold spare produce at the market. Markets sold food **staples** such as brown bread and a thick beer. The diet was simple. The Egyptians ate fish from the Nile, dried beans, fruit, and vegetables. Only the royal family and rich courtiers could afford to eat meat regularly.

Travel on the Nile

The Nile not only watered the land. It was also Egypt's main highway. The Egyptians did not have wheeled transport. They walked or used donkeys to carry goods on land. Other goods were transported by boat on the river.

Ordinary Egyptian tombs were hut-like structures called mastabas.

People, food, and goods were carried along the Nile by boat. Most of the huge stones used to build the Great Pyramid and the other pyramids were transported to Giza by boat.

SCIENCE SOLVES IT

Pharaoh Khufu's Boat

In 1954, archaeologists at Giza found the remains of solar barks, or boats. Boats were important in Egyptian life. The buried boats represented the sun, which the Egyptians saw as a boat crossing the sky. The boats were built to take Pharaoh Khufu to the **afterlife**. One boat was in more than 1,000 pieces. It had to be put together like a massive puzzle!

Who Did the Work?

Building the pyramids required many workers. Historians think it took at least 5,000 workers 20 years to build the Great Pyramid. Some of the workers were specialists, such as **architects** or surveyors. Most were seasonal workers. Farmers worked for the pharaoh when the Nile flooded and they could not work in the fields.

Working for the pharaoh was seen as an honor. Egyptians believed workers would have an easy voyage to the afterlife when they died. Specialists such as carpenters made tools, furniture, and sleds that were used to move heavy stones to the pyramid site. Metalworkers made tools, while potters made clay pots to hold water or to cook food on fires.

The workers were organized by many foremen and overseers. The most important person on the construction site was the pharaoh's personal architect. It was the architect's job to make sure the pyramid was built as the pharaoh wished. The pyramid had to be grand enough to ensure that the pharaoh had a smooth passage into the next life after his death.

Deir el-Medina was home to workers who built the royal tombs at Luxor.

What Did the Egyptians Believe About Death?

The pyramids are some of the most remarkable tombs ever built. They tell us a lot about what the ancient Egyptians thought about death.

The ancient Egyptians worshiped many gods. The people believed it was their duty to keep the gods happy. They also believed that life continued after death. For this reason, their bodies were carefully preserved after death. This process is known as **mummification**.

The first mummies were created naturally. **Ancestors** of the Egyptians had left dead bodies in the desert. They noticed that the bodies dried out as moisture soaked into the sand, and that the body remained preserved.

Mummies were wrapped in linen for burial. →

Ten-Week Process

In about 2600 BCE, the Egyptians came up with a way to copy natural mummification to prepare people for the afterlife. The process took about 10 weeks. First, special priests called **embalmers** removed the brain from the dead person. They pulled it out through the nose. Then they cut into the side of the body, and removed the stomach, liver, lungs, and intestines. They left the heart inside. The body was washed in water or wine. It was covered with natron, a type of salt that was found in the desert. The salt absorbed all the fluids from the body. It took about 40 days to dry the body out completely.

When it was dry, the body was covered with oil, wax, and resin (a sticky substance that comes from trees). Then the hollow bodies were packed with sand or cloth to give them a lifelike shape. Finally, the mummy was wrapped in layers of linen strips.

The richer the person, the more layers of linen were used to wrap the mummy. Special charms known as **amulets** were placed between the layers of linen. They were thought to protect the body on its journey to the afterlife.

After the final layer of linen had been wrapped around the body, the mummy was ready for burial. The head was covered with a mask and the mummy was put inside a decorated coffin. Sometimes there were several coffins one inside the other to give the mummy more protection. The outer coffin was made of stone. It was called a sarcophagus.

Skilled Priests

The priests who worked as embalmers were very skilled. They had to know all the special prayers and rituals that had to be performed at certain times during the process.

This gold mask →
covered the mummy of
Pharaoh Tutankhamun.

The priests also had to study the human body, so they knew where the internal organs were located.

Saving the Organs

The organs that were removed from the body were put in special containers known as canopic jars. Each jar had a head that represented a human or an animal to protect the contents. The ancient Egyptians believed that the dead person would need these organs in the afterlife, so the jars were buried with the body. The heart was left inside the body. People believed that the heart was the center of a person and their intelligence. It was so vital for the next life that it was never separated from the body.

Canopic jars were decorated with the heads of the sons of Horus, the god of the sky. From left to right: a jackal, a baboon, a falcon, and a human.

23

Expensive Process

Mummification took a long time. It was also expensive. Only the richest Egyptians could afford to be mummified. Their coffins were sometimes painted with images of the dead person meeting various gods. The images were intended to tell the soul of the dead person what he or she needed to do to make the journey to the afterlife.

The inside of this coffin is painted with images to help the dead person in the afterlife.

Poorer Egyptians could not afford to be mummified. Most were buried without coffins. They were simply wrapped in bandages and put in a tomb or buried in a hole in the ground.

Luxury Burials

Experts have found the mummies of many pharaohs and other important Egyptians. Most were discovered in the Valley of the Kings, where many pharaohs were buried. The tombs are decorated with wall paintings. The mummies lie inside sarcophaguses and wooden coffins. Some have masks of gold, and precious stones in their bandages.

Mummies found on a shelf in a tomb in the Valley of the Kings.

Missing Mummies

Because the pyramids are the largest tombs ever made, people have assumed for centuries that the mummies of the kings who built them must be somewhere inside. The bodies have proved difficult to find, however. So far no body has ever been found inside a pyramid.

Experts desperately want to discover a mummy from a pyramid, because mummies are one of their best sources of information about ancient Egypt. Thanks to modern technology, a mummy provides a glimpse of the time when its owner lived and died.

SCIENCE SOLVES IT

Learning About Mummies

Archaeologists use technology to unwrap the secrets of the mummies. **CAT** scanners produce 3D images of the bodies. Tiny cameras called endoscopes can show images of what is inside a mummy. One of the biggest breakthroughs came with **DNA** testing. Experts can use the dried skin and bone of the mummy to map its individual **genetic** code.

An American expert prepares a mummy from Peru for a scan.

↑ Some bandages used to wrap mummies were painted with images of the gods.

Scientific Examination

In the mid-1900s, scientists began to use **X-rays** to look inside mummies without having to unwrap them. They **dissected** bodies to find out how and why a person had died. They were able to analyze **organic** material on the body. **Pollen**, for example, shows what kind of plants were growing at the time a mummy was buried.

Today, experts take great care when unwrapping a mummy. They record everything and photograph it. They analyze every part of the mummy with the latest DNA tests. They can begin to reconstruct a mummy's whole life history.

Who Was Buried Inside the Pyramids?

No bodies have ever been found inside the pyramids. What became of the kings who built the monuments as their tombs?

Building a pyramid took thousands of workers many years to complete. Only the pharaoh could afford to have one built. As soon as a new pharaoh came to the throne, work began on building his tomb. It could take as long as 20 years to finish.

We know that the pharaohs who ordered the pyramids to be built intended to use them as tombs. Pharaoh Djoser built the first pyramid, the Step Pyramid in Saqqara. Djoser hoped the pyramid

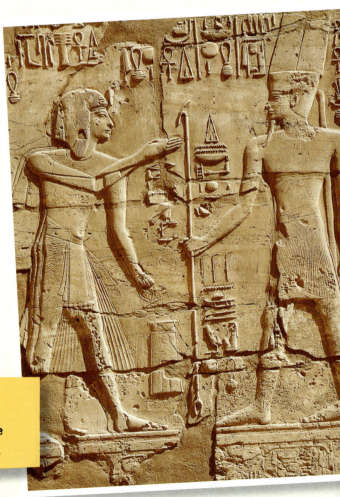

This pharaoh carries a rod as a symbol of his power. He also wears the crown of Egypt. →

would prevent his grave from being robbed of the possessions that were buried with him. He was buried in an underground chamber beneath the pyramid. Despite his precautions, his tomb was robbed after his death.

After Djoser, the next pharaoh to build a pyramid was Sneferu. In fact, he built three. The first was a step pyramid. The second was meant to have smooth sides, but construction went wrong. The builders had to change the angle of the sides to stop the structure falling down. Today, this is known as the Bent Pyramid. Sneferu's third pyramid was the first successful smooth-sided pyramid. But none of the three pyramids has been found to contain a mummy.

American Pyramids

Some peoples in Mesoamerica built pyramids. Unlike Egyptian pyramids, the buildings may have been used to follow the movements of stars and planets in the night sky. The pyramids were also used in ceremonies. They often had a wooden temple on top. Human **sacrifices** sometimes took place on top of pyramids. Experts think vcitims were killed there to keep the gods happy.

Empty Pyramids

The closest thing to a body to be found in a pyramid to date was a mummified foot found beneath Djoser's pyramid. The only other sign of any kind of burial in a pyramid was found in the smallest of the three pyramids at Giza. This pyramid belonged to Pharaoh Menkaure. It contained a damaged wooden coffin—but the coffin was empty.

This pyramid was built by the Maya at Tikal in Guatemala.

Vital Clues

How do experts know that the pyramids were the tombs of the pharaohs if no bodies have been found? One clue comes from the hieroglyphs carved or painted inside the pyramids or in the temples that were built near them. When Jean-François Champollion finally learned what the hieroglyphs meant in the 1820s, archaeologists could confirm that the pyramids were tombs. They also learned new information about who had built the pyramids.

In the second largest pyramid at Giza, archaeologists found an **inscription** that said "Great is Khafre." This finally confirmed that the pyramid had belonged to Khafre. In Menkaure's smaller pyramid archaeologists found an inscription reading "Menkaure is Divine."

These steps lead to tunnels beneath Khufu's Great Pyramid at Giza.
→

Missing Khufu

The Great Pyramid itself was built for the Pharaoh Khufu. No images of Khufu have ever been found there. The only known portrait of Khufu is a tiny statue carved from ivory. It measures just 3 inches (7.5 cm) tall. Experts find this surprising.

Khufu was one of the most powerful of all Egypt's rulers, but archaeologists have not found any inscriptions mentioning Khufu's name. Why was there no mention of this powerful pharaoh? Experts still do not know the answer to the mystery.

The mystery of Khufu's disappearance might soon be solved. The latest technology has helped experts to carry out more exploration inside tunnels of the Great Pyramid.

Secret Chambers

Does Khufu's mummy still lie somewhere inside the Great Pyramid? One of the most mysterious parts of the pyramid is the King's Chamber. The chamber is made from granite. Inside is a large sarcophagus, which is also made out of granite. The sarcophagus is the only **artifact** found inside the pyramid. It is empty.

The only way to reach the King's Chamber is through a long, narrow tunnel.

Were the mummies of the pharaoh and his wife both placed in the Great Pyramid? →

↑ After about 1500 BCE Egyptian rulers were buried in the Valley of the Kings.

SCIENCE SOLVES IT

Reconstructing the Past

Until the late 1900s, experts could only imagine how the pyramids looked when they were first completed. Now digital architects use computer-aided design to create 3D images of ancient monuments. Computer programs use thousands of separate measurements taken from the ruins to create an image of how the original site would have appeared. They can even reconstruct any missing parts to be as accurate as possible.

Arab explorers had found the passage in the ninth century CE when they first broke into the pyramid. Little more was discovered about the pyramid for over 1,000 years, but in 1993, a German scientist used a robot fitted with a camera to explore the pyramid's smallest tunnels.

Deep inside the pyramid, the camera "saw" hieroglyphs written in red paint. This was the first writing ever to be found inside the 4,500-year-old pyramid. But what did it say?

Experts are still not sure. They think some of the symbols might actually be the names of workers who helped to construct the pyramid.

The robot traveled as far as a mysterious door, but could go no farther. What lay behind the door? The answer came in 2002. Scientists used another robot to drill a tiny hole in the door.

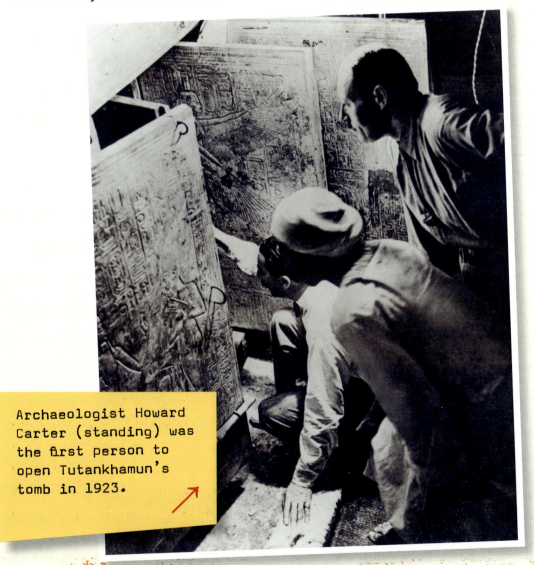

Archaeologist Howard Carter (standing) was the first person to open Tutankhamun's tomb in 1923.

They pushed a tiny camera through the hole. Inside was a small chamber blocked by another door. This door had what looked like metal handles, but they did not seem to have any purpose. So far, experts do not know what lies behind the second door. One mystery had been solved, but another remains.

The Last Pyramids

By around 1525 BCE, the pharaohs had stopped building huge pyramids to house their tombs. The last pyramids were poorly constructed. They were not as secure as the Great Pyramid and were therefore easy to rob.

Tutankhamun's tomb was piled full of gold, silver and precious objects.

Tutankhamun was buried in a gilded coffin (*left*) inside a gold sarcophagus (*right*).

A pyramid was like a signal to ancient robbers that a rich and important person was buried inside. This meant the tomb would also contain treasure. From around 1500 BCE, the pharaohs began to be buried in the Valley of the Kings near the city of Luxor. The tombs were dug deep into the rocky walls of the valley, so they were impossible to find.

Tutankhamun's Tomb

The most famous tomb in the Valley of the Kings belonged to a young pharaoh who died when he was just 19 years old. His name was Tutankhamun, and he ruled Egypt between 1336 and 1327 BCE. His tomb was found in 1922, and was opened the following year. The spectacular treasures it contained included a gold mask of the pharaoh, gold jewelry, weapons, clothing, furniture, and chariots. The discovery made experts wonder about the treasures that might have once been buried in the pyramids—or that might still be hidden somewhere inside them.

What's Left to Discover?

Thousands of years after they were built, many mysteries about the pyramids remain unsolved. Perhaps modern science will reveal some of the answers.

The first Arab explorers who dug into Khufu's Great Pyramid at Giza in 820 CE did not find any treasure. Since then, very few valuable objects have been found inside any pyramid. But that has not stopped explorers and other visitors from looking. They hope they might find undiscovered treasure.

In the past, treasure hunters did find artifacts at ancient sites. Usually, these artifacts were not financially valuable, but would be useful to historians. However, people did not always understand what they found. Many objects were treated badly. That destroyed information they might have revealed.

Since the pyramids were first discovered, ancient Egypt has fascinated people. This image is from a 1917 movie about the Egyptian queen Cleopatra.

Napoleon is shown during his visit to the Great Sphinx at Giza in this painting from 1886.

An Egyptian Craze

In 1798 and 1799, Emperor Napoleon Bonaparte of France led a campaign to conquer Egypt. The emperor took with him many scientists and artists. They cataloged everything they saw, and took many artifacts back to France. The French enthusiasm for ancient Egyptian culture soon began to spread. Within a few years, British and American archaeologists had also visited ancient sites and removed thousands of objects from Egypt.

Suddenly mummies were being displayed in museums in Europe and North America. In the early 1800s, some American museums sent their mummies on tour. Crowds gathered to see them and learn about them. People held parties where they unwrapped mummies' bandages. Most people unwrapping the mummies were not experts, and the mummies sometimes fell apart.

Other mummies were ground into powder, which was used to make artists' paint. When King Tutankhamun's tomb was found to be full of treasures in 1923, the discovery led to a new interest in the mysteries of ancient Egypt.

New Discoveries

Has everything been found? Experts estimate that only around a third of ancient Egypt's sites have been uncovered. No one knows what might be left to find. Archaeologists are particularly excited at the idea of finding human remains. Egypt's dry climate preserves organic material well. Human remains could easily still survive.

The entrance to Tutankhamun's tomb lies in the cliffs of the Valley of the Kings.

In 2016, experts discovered that another tomb might be hidden behind Tutankhamun's tomb in the

Valley of the Kings. They think the tomb might belong to Queen Nefertiti, the wife of Tutankhamun's father. The queen is one of the best-known ancient Egyptians. She was famous for her beauty.

Is It the Queen?

Archaeologists learned there might be a tomb behind the wall by using ground-penetrating **radar**. The plastered walls of Tutankhamun's tomb seem solid, but the radar shows that there are openings behind the west and north walls. Scans also show organic and metallic remains behind the walls. Experts believe that something was placed behind the walls and then deliberately hidden away.

The experts think the hidden tomb might belong to Queen Nefertiti. In the past, it was believed that the queen's mummy

Queen Nefertiti is portrayed in this famous Egyptian sculpture.

was in the Egyptian Museum in Cairo. But recent DNA tests have shown that the mummy in the museum is not Nefertiti. It belongs to Tutankhamun's mother, who was a royal servant.

Solving a Mystery

Science is helping solve mysteries from the past. One of the biggest mysteries about Tutankhamun was why he ruled for such a short time.

Should the British Museum give the Rosetta Stone to Egypt?

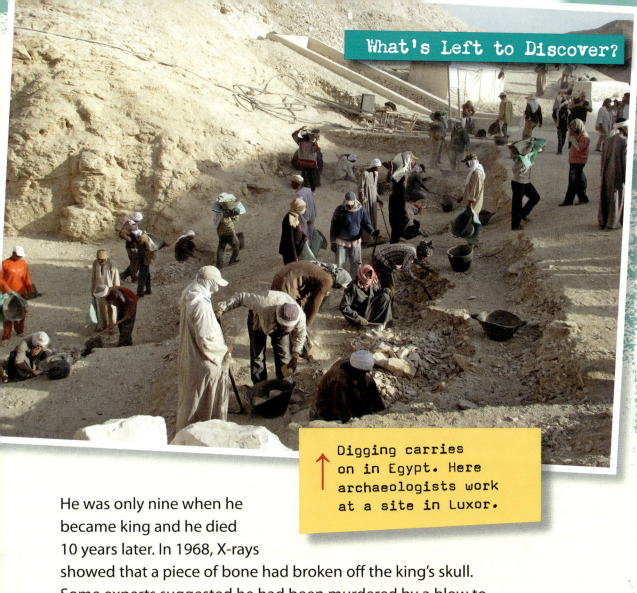

He was only nine when he became king and he died 10 years later. In 1968, X-rays showed that a piece of bone had broken off the king's skull. Some experts suggested he had been murdered by a blow to the head. In 2005, however, more detailed CAT scans showed the skull had been damaged after death. The damage may have been caused when the king's gold mask was removed.

The CAT scans also showed that the king had a broken thigh bone. This led to a suggestion that Tutankhamun had died as a result of falling from a **chariot**. Since then, experts have carried out more DNA studies on the mummy.

This is the 3D CAT scan taken of Tutankhamun in 2005.

Scientists now think that Tutankhamun died from complications from his broken leg and the effects of an infection. The infection was probably malaria. Tutankhamun's story has been rewritten as technology advances.

Recent Discoveries

Archaeologists continue to uncover Egypt's ancient sites. What do they hope to find? One exciting discovery came at Giza. Experts sent remote-controlled cameras inside the Great Pyramid. They also lowered tiny cameras into pits nearby. The cameras revealed the remains of a buried boat. It is likely another vessel intended to carry Khufu to the afterlife after his death. Meanwhile, mapping technology has revealed the ruins of a city that was once home to the pyramid builders. Dormitories, workshops, and cooking areas have been found. It seems that much remains to be discovered about ancient Egypt.

At night the pyramids are illuminated for tourists, but the stones still hide many secrets.

Glossary

afterlife Life after death.

amulets Small pieces of jewelry thought to protect against evil.

ancestors People in the past from whom someone is descended.

archaeologists People who study the past by examining old ruins, objects, and records.

architects People who design buildings.

artifact An object made by human beings, usually with a cultural or historical value.

capstone A pointed stone on the top of a pyramid.

CAT An abbreviation for computed, or computerized, axial tomography, a way of creating 3D scans.

chariot A two-wheeled vehicle pulled by a horse, usually used for fighting.

dissected Cut open in a methodical way.

DNA An abbreviation for deoxyribonucleic acid, the material by which parents pass on characteristics to their children.

drought A long period without any rain.

embalmers People who preserve bodies.

fertile Able to produce abundant crops and other vegetation.

genetic Relating to genes passed from parents to their children.

inscription Writing carved into a hard surface.

irrigate To artificially supply water to land in order to grow crops.

mummification The process of creating a mummy.

organic Related to things that are or have been alive.

pollen Powdery grains produced by plants.

radar A device for locating objects that sends out radio waves, which are reflected by objects and measured as they return to the device .

sacrifices Offerings to the gods, sometimes of living animals or people.

sarcophagus A stone coffin.

silt Sand or clay deposited by a river.

sphinx An imaginary creature with the body of a lion and the head of a human or animal.

staples Foods that are the main parts of people's diet.

vaulted Having an arched ceiling.

X-ray A wave that can pass through materials and that is used to make images of things that are usually hidden from sight.

Further Resources

Books

Deady, Kathleen W. *Ancient Egypt: Beyond the Pyramids*. Great Civilizations. Mankato, Minn: Capstone Press, 2012.

Hoobler, Thomas and Dorothy. *Where Are the Great Pyramids?* Where Are? New York: Grosset & Dunlap, 2015.

Morley, Jacqueline. *You Wouldn't Want to Be a Pyramid Builder*. Jobs You'd Rather Not Have. New York: Franklin Watts, 2014.

Rajczak, Kristen. *20 Fun Facts About the Great Pyramid*. Fun Fact File: World Wonders. New York: Gareth Stevens Publishing, 2014.

Websites

http://www.childrensuniversity. manchester.ac.uk/interactives/history/ egypt/
The Children's University site from the University of Manchester has a section on ancient Egypt, with an interactive panorama of the pyramids at Giza.

www.ducksters.com/history/ancient_ egypt/great_pyramid_of_giza.php
This Ducksters page features information about the Great Pyramid at Giza.

http://www.momjunction.com/articles/ facts-about-ancient-egyptian-pyramids- for-kids_00381425/#gref
Mom Junction has a list of facts about the pyramids and the people who built them, with links to many other pages.

http://www.ngkids.co.uk/history/ten- facts-about-ancient-egypt
National Geographic for Kids has 10 facts about ancient Egypt.

http://www.softschools.com/facts/ wonders_of_the_world/great_pyramid_ of_giza_facts/66/
This page from Soft Schools has a list of fascinating facts about the Great Pyramid.

Publisher's note to educators and parents: Our editors have carefully reviewed these websites to ensure that they are suitable for students. Many websites change frequently, however, and we cannot guarantee that a site's future contents will continue to meet our high standards of quality and educational value. Be advised that students should be closely supervised whenever they access the Internet.

Index

A
afterlife 18, 21, 23, 24
Al-Mamun, Caliph 9
Arabs 8, 10, 34, 38
architects 18, 19

B
Bent Pyramid 29
boats 18, 45
Bonaparte, Napoleon 39
British Museum 15, 42

C
Cairo 4, 5
canopic jars 23
capstones 5, 10
Carter, Howard 35
CAT scanners 26
Champollion, Jean-François 16, 31
Cleopatra VII 15, 38
computer-aided design 34

D
death, beliefs 20
Deir el-Medina 19
Demotic 13, 15, 16
Djoser 28–29
Djoser, Pharaoh 7, 30
DNA testing 26, 27, 42

E F
Egypt, unification of 14
embalmers 21, 22
farming 14, 16, 17
flood, annual 16, 17

G
Giza 4, 6, 18, 30, 31, 45

gods 6, 8, 20, 21
grave robbing 29, 37
Great Pyramid 5, 7, 9, 10, 11, 18, 31, 32–36, 37, 38, 45
Great Sphinx 6, 7, 39

H I
hieroglyphs 13, 15, 16, 31, 34
Imhotep 7
inscriptions 31
irrigation 16

K L
Khafre, Pharaoh 31, 32
Khufu, Pharaoh 11, 18, 32, 45
King's Chamber 10, 11, 33
Luxor 7, 37

M
mastabas 17
Maya 30
Menkaure, Pharaoh 30, 31
mummies 26, 27, 39, 40
mummification 20–25

N
Narmer, Pharaoh 14
Nefertiti 41, 42
Nile River 4, 5, 9, 12, 14, 16, 18

P Q
papyrus 13
pharaohs 6, 7, 17, 19, 25, 28
Ptolemy V, King 15
pyramids 4, 5, 6, 7, 8, 9, 10, 11, 28, 30, 31, 36
Queen's Chamber 10, 11

R
Ra 6, 8
radar 41
robots 34, 35, 45
Romans 15
Rosetta Stone 15, 16, 42

S
sacrifices, human 30
Saqqara 7, 28
sarcophagus 22, 33
Sea Peoples 15
Sneferu, Pharaoh 29
Step Pyramid 28–29
step pyramids 8

T
technology 26, 33, 34
temples 8, 9, 12
tombs 8, 17, 20, 25, 26, 31, 40, 41
trade 14
transportation 17, 18
treasure 37, 38
Tutankhamun 22, 35, 37, 40, 41, 42–44
Thutmose IV 7, 8

V W X
Valley of the Kings 7, 25, 34, 37, 40, 41
workers, construction 18, 19, 28, 45
writing, Egyptian 13, 15
X-rays 27